# A Season of Fruit

## Ian Pinto

Think Tank™
BOOKS

Title: A Season of Fruit
Author: Ian Pinto
Published by: Think Tank Books™ in 2020
Address: RZ-26/27B, Ashok Park, West Sagarpur, New Delhi - 110046
Website: thinktankbooks.com
Email: editorial@thinktankbooks.com



This is a work of fiction.

Printed at: Thomson Press
18/35 Delhi-Mathura Road, Faridabad, Haryana 121007

ISBN: 978-81-947561-3-2
Price: INR 125/-
Maximum retail price of this book listed is only for the Indian subcontinent. Selling price may vary elsewhere.

10 9 8 7 6 5 4 3 2 1

*Dedicated to my community at Don Bosco Sulcorna: Frs. Bernardino, Jacinto, Anisio, Allwyn and Constantine, Br. Frederick, and Cls. Clement, Joswin and Ashley, who shaped my experience there and have influenced the writing of this book in a big way.*

# ~~~About the Author~~~

Ian Pinto is a Salesian of Don Bosco (SDB) belonging to the Panjim-Konkan Province (INP). He is a prolific author of numerous articles that have featured in national magazines, journals and local dailies.

He has published an anthology of poems under the title Pen Downs (2019) and is currently pursuing a Bachelor of Theology degree as part of his formation to the Catholic priesthood. He enjoys music and living life to the full.

# ~~~Acknowledgement~~~

I would like to place on record my thanks to those people who have helped me in the publication of this book.

First and foremost, I would like to thank my parents for being open to the idea of publishing this book and for being willing to cover the cost of publication despite the current situation of economic difficulty.

I would like to thank the team at Think Tank Books for being gracious in designing the book and seeing to the layout and offering me guidance and help to ensure that the book is of good standard and attractive to all readers.

Finally, I would like to thank all those who helped and supported me over the course of the past year, my colleagues both Salesian and the staff of the Don Bosco School, Sulcorna and the students who brightened my days.

# ~~~Introduction~~~

I left my home soon after I completed my SSC to become a priest. I felt that God wanted me to become a priest and had put in my heart the desire to do so. This led me to the Salesian Society, which is composed of priests and consecrated laymen, who commit their lives to save souls, especially of young people. My journey in the Salesian society has been full of diverse experiences and challenges. Nobody said that life here would be easy and frankly, it has never been. Every year the challenges seemed to grow but so did the conviction and deepening of my vocation.

Every few years I found myself in a new setup designed to prepare me to become a good and effective Salesian. The last phase I completed was what we Salesians call Practical Training, more commonly known in clerical circles as Regency. That is the period in which a young candidate has to put into practice all that he has learnt in the preceding years of formation. It is designed to give the individual a firsthand experience of Salesian work and test their suitability for this way of life.

Since this is a phase of intense testing, many tend to fall out and leave the Society. I had very intense and challenging experiences during both my years of practical training. My experiences have been the inspiration for every poem in this book. Here, you will find the highs and lows that marked my final year of training at Don Bosco, Sulcorna. You will find my musings, my reflections, my doubts and my hopes laid bare.

The writing of this book has been a process of catharsis and has helped me deal with and confront a lot of my personal issues, attitudes and emotional baggage. I confess that the writing of each poem has brought healing to my mind and has helped me appreciate each experience and its educational and spiritual value. For this reason, I have called this book *A Season of Fruit*. Looking back now, I see how each experience has been like a seed that has borne fruit.

You will find here a variety of emotions and experiences, and nuggets of wisdom. I pray they help you on your journey in life.

## ~~~The Commission~~~

"Go," I was told
To a place I had known;
I was glad, I was bold
To make something of my own.

Here's a chance, let me grab;
Open heart and open mind;
Easy life is a drab
I'm getting out of this bind.

The field of work is vast
There is no time to wait around;
Get in the mould or break the cast?
That's the choice that's got me bound.

Rolled up sleeves and head bowed down
I push onward, storm or calm;
Others look with smile or frown
Each experience a new psalm.

The final goal is crystal clear
I've got hope to lift me up;
It's the journey that is drear
But I'm not giving up this cup.

Though the thorns pierce my feet
And the barbs strike at the heart

I'm not gonna let defeat
Discourage me from a new start.

I've got goals set to achieve
But there's something set to do
Obedience, however is the sieve
Got to accept what it lets through.

## ~~~Does This Work?~~~

Sitting back wondering
On all that could be different,
On all that was magnificent,
And what has turned irrelevant.

Why good has lost its spark,
While evil spreads its dark
Wings, Have I not left a mark
On lives that yearned for love and acceptance?

Could it really be
That it was all a dream?
From the start a hopeless scheme,
Something only God could redeem?

I worked, put blood and sweat,
It hurt but I don't regret,
'Cause I know I did my best
To raise the bar you set.

I've tried but I won't bet
You gained a level-head;
This pain is thoroughbred,
It's draining all my strength.

And yet I can't help thinking,
This experiment is working,

Because you are out there putting
To use what you have learnt here.

Would you be so kind
To take a little time
And recall sometimes to mind
The sacrifices gone behind.

I know it seems audacious
For me to claim what's precious
But you could make a difference
If only you'd make the effort.

## ~~~Played My Part~~~

There's a job I've got to do
And there's someone I've got to be;
In the mix, I find myself
Losing out on the real me.

There are things I've got to say
And decisions I have to make;
Often I find myself all alone
Wondering if it's the right path to take.

There are children put under me
And there are others for whom I care;
If I stray to show some love
Tell me why is it not fair?

There are places I have to be
And there are place I want to go;
Can I simply pull the brakes
On being significant and doing more?

There are people I have to meet
And there are people I want to know;
But I simply can't stand aside
As the opportunities flow.

There are things demanded
And there are things I wanted;

If I faithlessly left it be
I would be forever haunted.

There are things which weigh me down
And there are things which get me high;
These pitfalls can't keep me grounded
I was born to fly.

In all the things supposed to be
I know, I played my part.
In all the things expected of me
Perhaps, I lacked a full heart.

## ~~~Where are the Facts?~~~

The cat is out of the bag.
Judgment let her loose.
The what, how, when are still unclear,
Yet, the story makes the news.

There's table-talk and discussion,
On what transpired there;
Ironically, nobody really knows,
What went on and where!

The facts are all in disarray,
Still the villain is pointed out;
A jury would have its reservations,
But the judge has no shadow of doubt.

The judgment seat is crowded,
As judges line the door;
They think it's duty and favour,
Their ignorance to show.

The villain goes about,
Doing what he knows best;
When suddenly he finds himself,
Receiving results of an unprepared test.

The final judgment's declared,
Devoid of facts or feelings;

The villain writhes in pain,
While judges continue dealings.

There is no court of appeal,
The defence is seldom heard;
An execution for petty crimes,
Judges always have the last word.

### ~~~Sunflowers and Delight~~~

Sunflowers bloom in summer time,
Oh, what a delight to see!
Smartly dressed in glorious prime,
They stand out regally.

They worry not if someone sees them,
While bees suck them dry;
Never do they bend their stem,
Or throw a tantrum or cry.

They love the sunlight burning,
A party all day long;
Displaying endless yearning,
For night to run along.

The sunflowers I have planted,
Don't fail to bring a smile;
Reminding me I'm wanted,
And live a life of style.

# ~~~**Rumours**~~~

Soundless whispers echoing through,
Walls of empty chatter;
Knowledge and truth surreptitiously depart,
Leaving behind sterile matter.

Unfounded perceptions riot run,
Countless nothings are exchanged;
Tireless labour building poor reputations,
Prudence is all but estranged.

Dripping tongues fill thirsty ears,
Brining unconventional satisfaction;
The ignoble work of restless idlers,
Destined for mindless distraction.

Perturbing industrious do-gooders,
Tipping weightless scales;
Jubilantly casting slurs,
While throwing innocence on the rails.

Ferocious madness, have you no end?
Is there nothing to make you stop?
The lies within? What tender surprise!
A well-guarded tongue can ably close shop.

## ~~~**Hope**~~~


Can't figure out the right side of the bed.
I am hurt when I rise; my head feels like lead.
Every step feels like thorns pricking under my feet.
Don't know how to push on; I am beat.


Every day is a test and it's weighing me down.
If I can't find support, I fear I'll drown.
Is there anyone there to lend a hand?
I've lost my footing and I'm sinking in quicksand.


The monotony of routine is gnawing at my bones.
My back is breaking from carrying these live stones.
Masking pain with a smile is my daily fare.
And I can't seem to find anyone to care.


Everywhere I look I find deceit and blame.
Can't wait to make an exit from this frustrating game.
I need something to help me stay and put up a fight.
Hope is all I've got to help me through the night.

### ~~~Mr. Right~~~

With head above shoulders
And nose in the clouds,
Struts along Mr. Right;
With hawk-eye for faults
And elephant ears for talk,
He's quick to catch another's plight.

Caught often looking down
Seemingly lost in his world,
He passes unnoticed by;
But oh, in talk
How learned he sounds,
Without regard for truth or lie.

Another's mistakes
He cannot let go,
"How can they blunder so?"
You'd think he'd know
Of log and speck,
Some consideration he ought to show.

He often ponders
And makes comments,
On things beyond his knowledge;
To dominate
And subjugate,
It seems his birth privilege.

His battles are many
But scars are few,
The armour glistens with pride;
For all the bravado outside
Poor Mr. Right inside,
Is a teenager in a grown man's hide.

He needs the attention
And pride of place,
His power feeds his urge;
His litany of achievement
What pity their value,
Are fit not for song but for dirge.

Calm down Mr. Right
You have not the truth,
That prerogative is God's alone;
Here's my advice
I know you care not for,
Put a little humility in your tone.

# ~~~Losing My Mind~~~

I'm losing my mind
To the ignorance around,
I swear and I feel emotionally unsound.
Looking so desperately to unwind,
I'm losing my mind
I'm losing my mind

I'm losing my mind
To the apathy I face,
I'm tired of seeing just what a disgrace
My efforts have wrought while being so kind,
I'm losing my mind
I'm losing my mind

I'm losing my mind
To arrogance and pride,
And dealing with contrary to what I decide.
People might think I'm crazy and blind,
I'm losing my mind
Badly losing my mind

I'm losing my mind
But don't get me wrong,
Don't mistake it for weakness
I'm actually strong.
If this a rant you happen to find,
Then maybe it's you that has lost your mind!

### ~~~The Hope of Friendship~~~

I cling to hope with all,
With all the strength my heart can spell.
How can I go without,
Without someone whom I can tell?
Just what goes on within,
Within a mind and heart that's full.
Emotions flex under the strain,
The strain released to ease the pull.

Upon a dreary, boorish day,
Day that strikes a tender vein.
If there's no one left to share,
To share the sting of unwelcome pain.
Madness would soon be rife,
Be rife until it has its way.
Then no amount of directed care
Care could make a brighter day.

I hope with earnest for a friend,
A friend who can help me through,
Life's journey winding and arduous,
Arduous like the bamboo grew.
There's nothing like a friend,
A friend who supports and catches you;
Ever ready to help and guide,
Guide in times both bright and blue.

# ~~~Darkness Falls~~~

Darkness spreads his thick black cloak
Every hour from twilight to dawn
Creeping slowly hands withdrawn
Playing on fear, a morbid joke.

Current never seems to hold
Every time it blows or pours
Department can't fulfil its chores
Stranding people in misery untold.

Rustic life with all its flair
Stained with sense of uncertainty
Solutions seem to take eternity
Yet somehow without sense of despair

Every time that darkness falls
Kids cry out in anxiety
Acknowledging mute notoriety
As life temporarily stalls.
The darkness has a power
It soothes and yet excites
Lodges peace and restless sprites
Ruling while in sleep all cower.

### ~~~Pandemic Trauma~~~

Can't move out
Stuck inside
Virus raging
People died.
Getting worried
Take a breath
Not a war yet
Just a threat.

Lockdown called
Life shuts down
Sudden movement
Draws a frown
Got no work
Forget the pay
Might get worse
If not this way.

People congregate
Can't they hear?
Voices rising
Sounding fear.

Time is precious
Running fast
No point chasing

Things don't last.

Life's a gift
Not bought with cash
Take time, enjoy it
Don't just dash.
One fine day
The time will come
Pleasures no purpose
To a body numb.

Spend your time
With people you love
Do what's pleasing
To God above.

### ~~~**Holy Like Mary**~~~

Virgin Mother we give praise
Through month long festivity;
All the children voices raise
Beckoning Divine activity.

Holy Mary, Virgin pure
Fill us with your love so sweet;
Teach us trials to endure
Till one day in heaven we meet.

Ever Virgin, full of grace
Show us how to lend a hand;
Let not sin leave any trace
That we might before God pure stand.

Mary Mother of all people
May your Son's words our mind fill;
Let our hearts be always supple
Burning to do God's Holy Will.

Help of Christians, Mother of God
Lift us up each time we fall;
Let us never stay tight-jawed
While taking the Good News to all.

## ~~~Sunny Mornings~~~

I'm waking up to sunny mornings
Putting aside tired yawnings.
As the chirping chorus sings
Grateful smiles it always brings.

Heavy mist dragging its feet
Takes its time to beat retreat.
Caressing the land so sweet
Calming down the rushing heat.

Dogs are running wild and free
Rush to lick and greet me.
Barking up at every tree
Chasing thieving monkey.

Whispers heard in gentle breeze
Brushing up against the leaves.
Get to work like busy bees
Another day to whine or seize.

Mountains glisten in the sun
Hiding it sometimes for fun.
Letting water freely run
Giving praise to the Great One.

# ~~~Dancing to Liberation~~~

I can feel a wiggle within;
Let me try and get it out.
Every time I hear good music,
I just want to jump and shout.

Can't contain the enthusiasm;
My feet seem on their own.
Drop a beat and watch me blaze,
I do better when not alone.

I can come across as quiet;
That's just how I live my code.
Put me on a stage and watch me,
Pump the crowd, have fun, explode!

I may not have grace or rhythm
But I know to have some fun.
Let me entertain with madness,
Ease up on my smoking gun.

Realize I'm not self-conscious;
I killed that a long time back.
Now I find that dancing helps me,
Keep my body and mind on track.

## ~~~Losing Out!~~~

I'm losing out on certain things.
I'm losing power in both my wings.
I'm losing touch with who I am.
I'm losing space to senseless spam.
I'm losing smiles to angry frowns.
I'm losing colour on my gowns.
I'm losing out on liberty.
I'm losing creativity.
I'm losing life I want to spend.
I'm losing things I often lend.
I'm losing out on making friends.
I'm losing time to make amends.
I'm losing my mind bit by bit.
I'm losing health and growing unfit.

I'm losing plenty that is true.
But now I'm losing something new.

I'm losing negativity.
I'm losing slowly jealousy.
I'm losing pride and that's no joke.
I'm losing anger though I choke.
I'm losing grip on grudges past.
I'm losing fear really fast.
I'm losing pleasure in my name.
I'm losing petty need for fame.
I'm losing thirst to be the best.

I'm losing urgency for rest.
I'm losing slowly feeling stress.
I'm losing need of fancy dress.

I'm losing poor attitude.
I'm gaining Divine gratitude.

## ~~~Do I Know You?~~~

Excuse me, how are you?
And when is your departure due?
You live here! I'm sorry,
Thought that was just a story.

It's true that you bathe here
And work and live in good cheer?
You eat at table with me?
But how come I never see?

Are you who you say you be?
Is that you really?
To me it seems all a charade,
A memory that'll slowly fade.

Don't get me wrong, you've done some work.
Responsibility you sometimes shirk.
I thought you were a busybody
Not trying just to be somebody.

It's hard you say then buckle up.
Didn't you choose to drink this cup?
So what if I squeeze vinegar?
Drink it like its sweet sugar.

Tell me, are you at your best?
Have you put your skills to test?

Are you charming and effective?
I'd diss you but I'm selective.

Did you know in my days
Things went always my ways?
I have done more than you could
It doesn't matter if I'm not any good.

I have built a foundation
That allows me constant vacation.
Do a little, then some rest,
You don't like it, be my guest.

Why are you not at your post,
Assisting like a damn ghost?
I don't care how it makes you feel;
See you at the next meal.

Don't tell me that your life is tough.
You haven't had it like me, rough.
My higher ups had given me hell
And here I barely tap your shell.

Don't act all different now and pout.
I told you what I heard about.
We share a roof and vocation too
But I don't know the real you!

### ~~~Make A Wish~~~

Annual day comes 'round again;
There's wonder and discussion.
Teacher's make a list of three;
Musical's the selection.

The pool of choice is booming;
Kids capacity needs test.
The challenge is accepted;
It's Aladdin for the best.

Work begins in full earnest;
Costumes, dance and stage décor.
Actors learn their parts by heart;
Promising a splendid show.

Hours and hours of work gone in;
Aimed at setting precedent.
Driven practice on and on;
Making children confident.

The day arrives in cat's shoes;
Campus alive in a buzz.
Opening song booms loudly;
Rising applause makes a fuzz.

Performers pack a strong punch;
Creativity in bloom.

Grand success in every smile;
Not a doubt in the packed room.

### ~~~Genie Magic~~~

Rub a lamp and make a wish,
The genie is here to serve;
Such desirable fantasy,
Striking a sensitive nerve.

Three wishes; whatever you like,
Sounds generous in good measure;
Be great, be awesome, be utterly forgettable,
It's entirely your pleasure.

Just say the words and you shall see,
Your wish come fully true;
The genie rolls his hands and whoosh!
There stands a brand new you!

Genie magic puts a mask,
On who you truly are;
It sets the stage and pins the light,
On YOU—the real star.

Why work your way to something good,
When all you need is wish?
'Cause real goals are never served,
By a maître d' on a dish.

## ~~~Kaleidoscope Views~~~

Inquiring eyes put out a scan.
Adoring eyes scream, "I'm a fan!"
Friendly eyes inquire, "How are you?"
Commanding eyes demand you do!
Tired eyes beg simply for rest.
Negative eyes put all to the test.
Happy eyes brighten the day.
Wise eyes show lost one's the way.
Peaceful eyes exude waves of calm.
Loving eyes feel like a soothing balm.
Hopeful eyes dream of greater good.
Hungry eyes constantly look for food.
Curious eyes beg to tell them more.
Rolling eyes shout, "You are a bore!"
Distracted eyes glance all over the place.
Perfect eyes complete a beautiful face.
Cheeky eyes long to make a scene.
Staring eyes are simply mean.
Downcast eyes are hiding something.
Forgiving eyes hold back nothing.

Every pair communicating,
Each a message is relating.
Eyes are more than tools to see,
They set apart humanity.

# ~~~Stubborn Stones~~~

Stubborn stones don't lie there still,
You'll find yourself soon rolling downhill.
Stubborn stones why do you sigh?
Right, of course, the grapes are high!

Stubborn stones the sun will burn you,
Its heat is strong if only you knew.
Stubborn stones your colour has gone;
You still look dull first thing in the morn.

Stubborn stones why won't you listen?
You know, someday you could end up in prison.
Stubborn stones what do you seek?
A pat on the back or a slap on the cheek?

Stubborn stones when will you see
That you were born to be happy and free?
Stubborn stones don't throw in the towel;
Put on a smile and take of that scowl.

Stubborn stones there's a long way to go.
Make your own path; Don't roll with the flow!
Stubborn stones don't chase butterflies;
Aim for the moon and shoot for the skies.

Stubborn stones the mud ain't your home;
You could mark a tomb or head a dome.

Stubborn stones mind what come out of your mouth;
It could make things better or send it south.


Stubborn stones grow smooth and smart;
Don't simply wish but cross your heart.
Stubborn stones live life purposefully
And you will be blessed eternally.


Stubborn stones the night has passed;
The day of judgment is approaching fast.
Stubborn stones pull up your socks;
You'd best ride the wave lest you end on the rocks.


Stubborn stones make up your mind;
Through hard work alone happiness you'll find.
Stubborn stones remember in poverty or wealth;
There's no greater treasure than health.


Stubborn stones wisdom learns from mistakes;
The bigger the jackpot the higher the stakes.
Stubborn stones don't let time pass you by;
Unless you don't mind to waste life and cry.

# ~~~Knowledge~~~

'To know.' What power lies therein;
A seed that can change the world.
Vast potential humbly lies,
Inside uncomfortably curled.

But power can be evil or good,
Depending on its use;
While some products demand our praise,
Others have no excuse!

Knowledge makes us human beings,
We wear it as prized gold;
All the while we build on it,
Firm foundations make strongholds.

Offering a life of hope,
The future on it depends;
Innovation comes not from giving up,
But finding ways 'round dead ends.

Knowledge makes the world go round,
Without it no life could be;
We often take for granted but
It's God's gift to us for free.

### ~~~A Gentleman~~~

What goes into making a man?
There's so much, it's unfair to constrict,
Well there definitely has to be a plan,
That's followed with discipline rather strict.
Doing one's duty without oversee or praise,
Lending ear to correction whenever the need;
Innovative and flexible in trying new ways,
Never tiring of positivity in thought, word and deed.
Polite and gentle in social dealing,
Going beyond limiting walls of discrimination;
Moved to decision by deep thought not mere feeling;
While staying reserved from ostentation.
The world is in need of real good men.
It's a reality each boy can make happen.

## ~~~Miraculous Lady on the Mount~~~

Holding on a sliver of hope,
Feeling faith rise again,
Pushing up to wearisome odds,
Daring to look beyond the pain.

Raising hopeful eyes to heaven,
Wishing on a miracle,
Praying to the Ever-Virgin,
Leaving worry skeptical.

Trusting in an intervention,
Fighting hard to live and cope,
Spreading her saving mantle,
Safeguarding all who dare to hope.

Waiting on a change of heart,
Teaching acts of surrender,
Thwarting Satan's devious plans,
Bringing back what's asunder.

Offering a brilliant witness,
Serving always Divine Son,
Extending tender open arms,
Keeping aside no one.

## ~~~Legacy~~~

The end is here,
My time has come;
Pack up to leave,
The job is done.

The roller coaster,
Grinds to a halt;
It starts to end,
Simply default.

I choose to ride,
The end in sight;
Will not leave shy,
But burning bright.

A life of candor,
Some show distaste;
Unsavory remarks,
Won't change me in haste.

I've got a heart,
I choose to show;
Won't break other hearts,
The rules I know.
Fashioned marvels,
All have seen;
Without an ear,

To what had been.

Inspiring novel ideas,
And fancy displays;
Serving up pleasures,
On Silver-lined trays.

A friendly presence,
A smiling face;
A lively name,
Around the place.

Welcome guest,
In any group;
Yet insufficient somehow,
In boarding troop.

Charming teacher,
Taking decisions bold;
Unwrapping talents,
Like hidden gold.

What legacy?
A mispronounced name;
I bet you I didn't,
Leave the place the same.

### ~~~Cool Dip in Summer~~~

Deny me not this little joy,
Of finding coolness in gentle stream,
As sun blares out all pleasant coy
Bringing discomfort with stern beam.
Aboard the wind come waves of heat,
Insalubrious sweat gushes forth,
I follow a path with stumbling feet,
To a pool concealed by undergrowth.
At last, respite from torturous burning,
Cool water chills my bones,
This welcome dip fulfils a yearning,
To lay back to ebbing quiet tones.
Refreshed I rise to greet the heat,
Pledging a return once more the summer to beat.

## ~~~Christmas Spirit~~~

It's Christmas! But the bells aren't ringing,
The boys in angelic choirs are singing,
Carols to the new-born babe,
Lying sweetly in a man-made stab'e.

Excitement turns the air around,
While love each one and work surround,
With hints of jealousy amid miserliness,
Is there place at Christmas for surliness?

Boys get busy their tasks to take,
Before they leave all ready to make,
But there are some who spoil the broth,
Spitting falsehood with mouth of froth.
Suddenly it's palpable, the Christmas spirit dips,
The walls are bare but for Christmas coloured strips,
Yet plenty remains but the boys are all gone,
There's hardly a day or two before the baby is born!

It's green and brown in Christmas town,
Some see lack of spirit, and frown,
So what if decorations fall,
One ought to heed the inner Christmas call!

# ~~~A Witness to Death~~~

The sudden news at breakfast time,
A man has lost his life,
Leaving behind three kids and a wife,
It's strange to hear funeral bells chime.

A rush to gather family,
And documents of death,
Leaving all so out of breath,
A teary-eyed assembly.

No hospital at stones throw,
Nor access to quite some facilities,
Except for basic utilities,
One must to the town go.

Victim to a rustic system,
Heart gave out and failed,
Even as the family wailed,
As people lined up to with them.

A man has left this world,
His family incomplete,
Caretakers the case insensitively treat,
In closed circle, unfair comments hurled.

Does it matter, what's not said?
Who was thanked and who was praised?

The family is clearly dazed,
A man they loved is dead!

**~~~A Brilliant Tour~~~**

A golden chance was offered,
Leave town for a couple of days,
Enjoy a sight-seeing tour,
Don't mind the hotel stays.

A long and tiresome journey,
Pickled with loads of fun,
Meeting people, making new friends,
While always on the run.

Drinking deep at the fount of beauty,
Taken up with the cultural shift,
Never mind the kids who share the room,
Who have no real sense of thrift.

The journey's winding and endless,
An impressive agenda to keep,
The comforts of stress-free living,
Ensure a good nights sleep.

Won't tire of the luxury,
And taste of select food,
Can't help but daily praise the Lord,
For this opportunity so good!

Exploited every scope for joy,
While keeping spirits high,

Enjoying the thrill of friendship and freedom,
Without rush to wave goodbye.

A little detour from schedule,
Turned acquaintances to friends,
The dream life slowly fades away,
To memory the ordinary blends.

### ~~~**Mary on the Mount**~~~

Miraculous statue of our Mother,
Bringing hope to all the sick,
Standing tall above all other,
Carrying prayers on every wick.

Serenely gazing on the land,
Immense gift of generous men,
Caring for the Salesian band,
Showing the way to heaven.

Undeterred by evil intent,
Healing all who come in faith,
Mediatrix of grace potent,
Line missing

Mary always be our guide
Though we falter, don't leave our side.

### ~~~Slander~~~

Why this urge to spoil a name?
Speak of what others do?
Is it just to cast blame
Or just cud that one must chew?

Does it profit anyone,
To cast a slur on one's neighbor?
'Cause when all is set and done,
Each reaps according to labour.

I dare not point a finger,
At any person but me,
For often my thoughts linger,
On the faults of he and she.

Do I not let my tongue slip,
On the misgivings of others?
And every time does that not rip,
A part of my sisters and brothers?

### ~~~Monsoon Gales~~~

Dark clouds gather,
Heavy with wet matter;
Beneath the mountains cower,
Ready for the impending shower.

Animals run for cover,
As Earth welcomes her lover;
Strong winds sweep through the land,
While thunder plays his band.

The breeze blows cold and hard,
Healing what's been marred;
Unsettling the dust,
Easing pressure on the crust.

With passion in its force,
Pushing obstacles on its course,
The gales herald the rain,
The monsoon they sustain.

Their ferocity blow out the light,
Their velocity a show of might;
The monsoon gales blow loud their horn,
And wipe away all that is worn.

**~~~Give Me A Break~~~**

Please spare me a moment to breathe,
I'm in desperate need.
Oh, will somebody heed?

I've got this heavy load on my chest,
And I think that it's best,
If I get some rest.

Right now I can't feel my feet,
My body is beat,
But there's no time to retreat.

There's a job that I've got to get done,
The responsibility can't shun,
Before I can have fun.

My mind is growing heavy and dull,
I'm in a steady mull,
End result seems null.

Every day brings its own set of pain,
I parade and there's rain,
My energy is on the wane.

How I long for the day to be free,
Spend some time mid the tree,

Do what satisfies me.

I don't care if it makes me seem less,
These feelings I can't suppress,
I just need to de-stress.

**~~~The Joy of Music~~~**

God bless the ones who made joyful noise,
Who ventured to let the heart speak,
And by their madness brought endless joy,
To all who pleasure deeply seek.

Music brings joy and tears in turn,
A melody for every emotional stop,
Its power uncanny to inspire a mood,
Can't help but twitch every time the beat drop.

Every word of every song an emotional sell,
Music carries life to life,
Its entertaining power is fit to be admired,
For lovers its absence cuts like a knife.

Music can brighten up the darkest day,
And help ease emotional pain,
For different people music holds different values,
But for me it's what keeps me sane.

### ~~~Picture Perfect Sunsets~~~

Whip out a camera and snap up the sky,
The sight will bring pleasure to the eye.
Clouds arranged picturesquely,
Stars shining coquettishly,
Birds chirping melodiously,
Hills gazing dazedly.

The sun like a painter colours the sky,
Each day seems to find a new shade of dye.
Sights simply amaze,
Inviting deep gaze,
Despite evening haze,
An aesthetic phase.

Waiting for sunset to take in the sky,
Can't help but smile as the sun passes by.
Descend in grace,
Stars fixed in place,
Darkening earth's face,
Leaving no trace.

### ~~~Divine Mercy~~~

Divine Mercy fall on us,
Fill our hearts with forgiveness.
Let us not hold grudges tight,
Leave us not in sin's wilderness.

Divine Mercy hear our prayer,
Help our failing faith to rise.
For our sake the cross you bore,
And paid on it the ultimate price.

Divine Mercy fill our hearts,
Let your love for us suffice.
Let our words by uplifting,
From our lips escape no lies.

Divine Mercy show the way,
Help us trust in you alone.
Healing bring to troubled hearts,
Through our lives your glory shown.

## ~~~Jungle Roads~~~

Jungle roads run wild and deep,
Traversable by tractor and jeep;
But if you choose to walk those ways,
You'd be walking along for days!

Jungle roads run high and low,
Over hills and rivulet flow;
Just know this, it's jungle track,
You'd do well to look over your back.

Jungle roads run smooth and rough,
Build endurance, make one tough;
Numerous ways to a destination,
Each one suiting an inclination.

Jungle roads run trodden or neglected,
Some appear promising while other leave you dejected,
The sights are great and the walks rewarding,
Every new discovery comes from prodding.

### ~~~A Salted Sky~~~

The sky is bright with a million lights,
A million stars that shine so bright.
Every night I gaze to the sky,
And am met with this brilliant sight.

The moon performs her daily dance,
The salted sky her stage,
As stars twinkle endlessly to no tune at all,
A masterpiece on a black page.

I gaze above with bated breath,
Awestruck by heavenly delight,
And for brief moments I find relief,
From all my mundane plight.

The salted sky rains down on me,
Hope in every shine.
In every arrangement a reminder that,
In the end things will turn out fine.

# ~~~Mind Your Attitude~~~

Don't flex your muscles very soon,
The audience has barely settled in;
When you're angry you're like a chest-thumping
baboon,
Don't you tire from the sound of your own din?

I'm sure you're great; you've shown some spark,
Spare me the talks of 'if I had been;'
The ego-boosting, heart-bashing topic is dark,
You deal with anger like a moody girl of thirteen.

You have got a great way of getting things done,
Mastered sweet talk and emotional sway;
The sudden mood swings though often stun,
Making others think twice before coming your way.

The 'don't give a damn' about repercussions,
Could prove costly in relational matters;
Confrontation cannot trump discussions,
They always leave truth and love in shatters.

You've got potential, there's no denying that,
Someday you'll make a huge splash wherever you sit;
But now you've got to check your ego growing fat,
That attitude has a lot to do with it.

### ~~~Let's Do Something~~~

Well the weather is great,
Let's go out and change our fate.
You've got other things to do?
That's alright, I'll take the cue.

I'm urging for a thrill,
Not simply a trek uphill.
Don't care for gimmicks and for drive,
I want more than just to survive.

Are you with me on this quest?
I can't promise you the best.
But I know it will be fun,
To spend our days in happy sun.

Don't let fear creep inside,
Find someone you can confide.
There'll be tension on the way,
The current will force you to sway.

Oh! That's not your cup of tea?
You are mindful of the fee.
Why so scared to have a ball?
When you try you sometimes fall.

Don't try simply to impress,
That always turns out a mess.

Shake off unhealthy opinion,
Or you'll turn into a minion.

Come live a little,
With care let's fiddle.
Won't upset the cart,
Nor break anyone's heart.

Without endangering innocence,
Or scope for improper inference.
Let's do something nice,
And let that desire suffice.